LISA BRUCE is a successful children's author, and a librarian at St Martin's
Teacher Training College in Ambleside. She has been a reviewer for *The Bookseller*,
a publishers' reader and a researcher for the Library Association.
Her previous titles include *Jazeera in the Sun* (Methuen), *Amazing Alphabets*
(Frances Lincoln), *Engine, Engine*, the Pix & Pax series and *Fran's Flower* which
was shortlisted for Sheffield Children's Book Award (all Bloomsbury).

ROBIN BELL CORFIELD studied Painting at Norwich School of Art and took a PGCE
at Reading University. He taught for many years before becoming a full-time illustrator.
His previous titles include *The Bloomsbury Book of Lullabies, Feather Pillows*
and *Our Field* (HarperCollins), A. E. Housman's *A Shropshire Lad* (Walker)
and *All the Year Round*, an anthology of poems (OUP).

To Roz Carlton, Liam, Carla and Jack – L.B.

For Ruth – R.B.C.

Row Your Boat

Lisa Bruce • Robin Bell Corfield

FRANCES LINCOLN

Row, row, row your boat .
Gently down the stream.
Merrily, merrily, merrily, merrily,
Life is but a dream.

Row, row, row your boat
Quickly up the river.
When the wind blows very hard,
We'll begin to shiver.

Row, row, row your boat
On the silvery lake.
If a wave comes rolling by,
Our little boat will shake.

Row, row, row your boat
Swiftly out to sea.
Can you see the pretty fish
Swim from you to me?

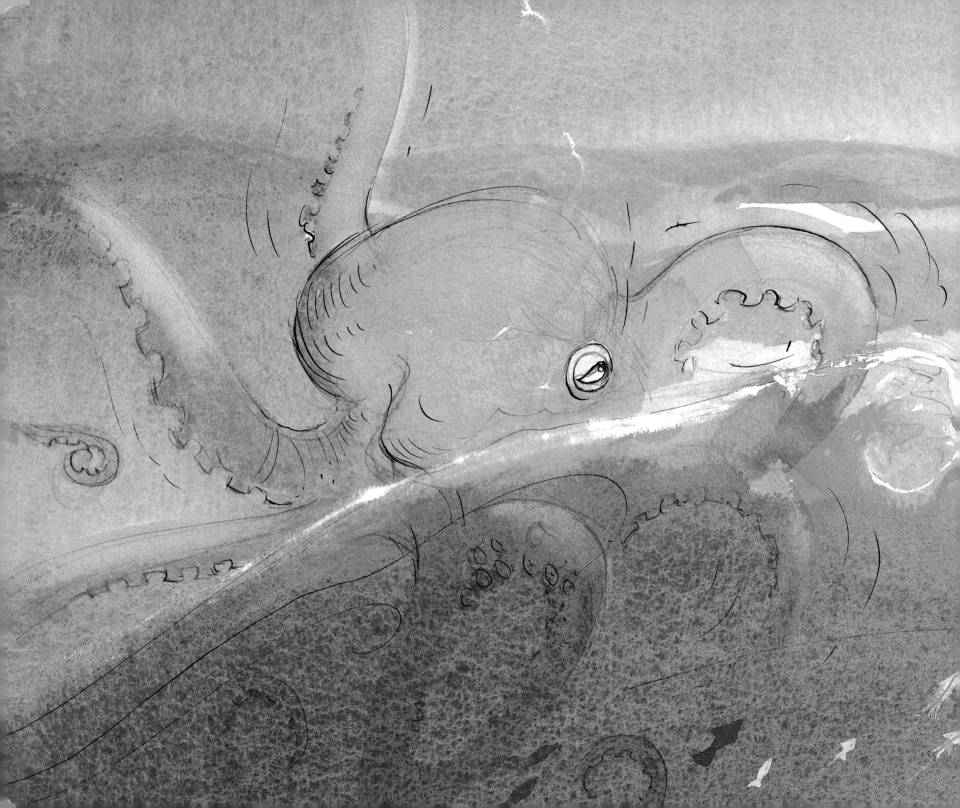

Row, row, row your boat
Across the ocean wide.
See the eight-legged octopus
Swim away and hide.

Row, row, row your boat
Slowly up the stream.
If you see a crocodile,
Don't forget to scream.

Row, row, row your boat
Home on the lagoon.
If you look up to the sky,
You will see the moon.

Row, row, row your boat
Sitting on the floor.
Are you getting tired now,
Or shall we sing once more?

Act Out the Rhyme!

Row, row, row your boat
Gently down the stream.
Merrily, merrily, merrily, merrily,
Life is but a dream.

Row, row, row your boat
Quickly up the river.
When the wind blows very hard,
We'll begin to shiver.

Row, row, row your boat
On the silvery lake.
If a wave comes rolling by,
Our little boat will shake.

Row, row, row your boat
Swiftly out to sea.
Can you see the pretty fish
Swim from you to me?

Row, row, row your boat
Across the ocean wide.
See the eight-legged octopus
Swim away and hide.

Row, row, row your boat
Slowly up the stream.
If you see a crocodile,
Don't forget to scream.

Row, row, row your boat
Home on the lagoon.
If you look up to the sky,
You will see the moon.

Row, row, row your boat
Sitting on the floor.
Are you getting tired now,
Or shall we sing once more?

Music for the Rhyme

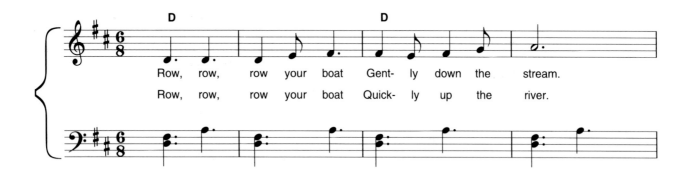

Row Your Boat copyright © Frances Lincoln Limited 2001
Text copyright © Lisa Bruce 2001. Illustrations copyright © Robin Bell Corfield 2001
Music arranged by Margaret Lion

First published in Great Britain in 2001 by Frances Lincoln Limited,
4 Torriano Mews, Torriano Avenue, London NW5 2RZ

ISBN 0-7112-1557-X hardback
ISBN 0-7112-1750-5 paperback

Printed in Hong Kong

3 5 7 9 8 6 4 2

MORE PICTURE BOOKS AVAILABLE IN PAPERBACK FROM FRANCES LINCOLN

FIDDLE I FEE

Jakki Wood

This exuberant, noisy book, based on the traditional nursery rhyme,
will have children shouting out animal noises at each turn of the page.

Suitable for Nursery Education and for National Curriculum English – Reading, Key Stage I

Scottish Guidelines English Language – Reading, Level A

ISBN 0-7112-0860-3

THE HOUSE THAT JACK BUILT

Jenny Stow

This familiar nursery rhyme is brought to life in a splendid Caribbean setting.

Suitable for Nursery Education and for National Curriculum English – Reading, Key Stage I

Scottish Guidelines English Language – Reading, Level A

ISBN 0-7112-1455-7

ELLIE'S GROWL

Karen Popham

Ellie loves it when her brother reads her books about animals, because he makes wonderful animal noises.
One day, Ellie learns that she, too can growl like a tiger – with some quite unexpected results!

Suitable for Nursery Education and for National Curriculum English – Reading, Key Stage I

Scottish Guidelines English Language – Reading, Levels A and B

ISBN 0-7112-1505-7